Citadel

Citadel

by Algis Budrys

Start Publishing PD LLC
Copyright © 2024 by Start Publishing PD LLC

Start Publishing PD is a registered trademark of Start Publishing PD LLC
Manufactured in the United States of America

Cover art: Shutterstock/Taisiya Kozorez

Cover design: Jennifer Do

10 9 8 7 6 5 4 3 2 1

ISBN 979-8-8809-0316-0

The aging man was sweating profusely, and he darted sidelong glances at the windowless walls of the outer office. By turns, he sat stiffly in a corner chair or paced uneasily, his head swiveling constantly.

His hand was clammy when Mead shook it.

"Hello, Mr. Mead," he said in a husky, hesitant voice, his eyes never quite still, never long on Mead's face, but darting hither and yon, his glance rebounding at every turn from the walls, the floor, the ceiling, the closed outer door.

Christopher Mead, Assistant Undersecretary for External Affairs, returned the handshake, smiling. "Please come into my office," he said quickly. "It's much more spacious."

"Thank you," the aging man said gratefully and hurried into the next room. Mead rapidly opened the windows, and some of the man's nervousness left him. He sank down into the visitor's chair in front of Mead's desk, his eyes drinking in the distances beyond the windows. "Thank you," he repeated.

Mead sat down behind the desk, leaned back, and waited for the man's breathing to slow. Finally he said, "It's good to see you again, Mr. Holliday. What can I do for you?"

Martin Holliday tore his glance away from the window long enough to raise his eyes to Mead's face and then drop them to the hands he had folded too deliberately in his lap.

"I'd—" His voice husked into unintelligibility, and he had to begin again. "I'd like to take an option on a new planet," he finally said.

Mead nodded. "I don't see why not." He gestured expressively at the star chart papered over one wall of his office. "We've certainly got plenty of them. But what happened with your first one?"

"It d-d-duh—"

"Mr. Holliday, I certainly won't be offended if you'd prefer to look out the window," Mead said quickly.

"Thank you." After a moment, he began again. "It didn't work out," he said, his glance flickering back to Mead for an instant before he had to look out the window again.

"I don't know where my figuring went wrong. It didn't go wrong. It was just ... just things. I thought I could sell enough subdivisions to cover the payments and still keep most of it for myself, but it didn't work out."

He looked quickly at Mead with a flash of groundless guilt in his eyes. "First I had to sell more than I'd intended, because I had to lower the original price. Somebody'd optioned another planet in the same system, and I hadn't counted on the competition. Then, even after I'd covered the option and posted surety on the payments, there were all kinds of expenses. Then I couldn't lease the mineral rights—" He looked at Mead again, as though he had to justify himself. "I don't know how that deal fell through. The company just ... just withdrew, all of a sudden."

"Do you think there might have been anything peculiar about that?" Mead asked. "I mean—could the company have made a deal with the colonists for a lower price after you'd been forced out?"

Holliday shook his head quickly. "Oh, no—nothing like that. The colonists and I got along fine. It wasn't as though I hadn't put the best land up for sale, or tried to make myself rich. Why, after I'd had to sell some of the remaining land, and I knew it wasn't worth staying, any more, some of them offered to lend me enough money to keep fifty thousand square miles for myself." He smiled warmly, his eyes blank while he focused on memory.

"But that wasn't it, of course," he went on. "I had my original investment back. But I couldn't tell them why I couldn't stay. It was people—even if I never saw them, it was the thought of people, with aircraft and rockets and roads—"

"I understand, Mr. Holliday," Mead said in an effort to spare him embarrassment.

Holliday looked at him helplessly. "I couldn't tell them that, could I, Mr. Mead? They were good, friendly people who wanted to help me. I couldn't tell them it was people, could I?"

He wet his dry lips and locked his eyes on the view outside the window. "All I want, Mr. Mead, is half a planet to myself," he said softly.

He shook his head. "Well, it'll work out this time. This time, I won't have to sell so much, and I'll have a place to spend what time I've got left in peace, without this ... this—" He gestured helplessly in an effort to convey his tortured consciousness of his own fear.

Mead nodded quickly as he saw his features knot convulsively. "Of course, Mr. Holliday. We'll get you an option on a new planet as quickly as we can."

"Thank you," Holliday said again. "Can we ... can we handle it today? I've had my credit transferred to a local bank."

"Certainly, Mr. Holliday. We won't keep you on Earth a moment longer than absolutely necessary." He took a standard form out of a desk drawer and passed it to Holliday for his signature.

"I'll be smarter this time," the aging man said, trying to convince himself, as he uncapped his pen. "This time, it'll work out."

"I'm sure it will, Mr. Holliday," Mead said.

Marlowe was obese. He sat behind his desk like a tuskless sea lion crouched behind a rock, and his cheeks merged into jowls and obliterated his neck. His desk was built specially, so that he could get his thighs under it. His office chair was heavier and wider by far than any standard size, its casters rolling on a special composition base that had been laid down over the carpeting, for Marlowe's weight would have cut any ordinary rug to shreds. His jacket stretched like pliofilm to enclose the bulk of his stooped shoulders, and his eyes surveyed his world behind the battlemented heaviness of the puffing flesh that filled their sockets.

A bulb flickered on his interphone set, and Marlowe shot a glance at the switch beneath it.

"Secretary, quite contrary," he muttered inaudibly. He flicked the switch. "Yes, Mary?" His voice rumbled out of the flabby cavern of his chest.

"Mr. Mead has just filed a report on Martin Holliday, Mr. Secretary. Would you like to see it?"

"Just give me a summary, Mary."

Under his breath he whispered, "Summary that mummery, Mary," and a thin smile fell about his lips while he listened. "Gave him Karlshaven IV, eh?" he observed when his secretary'd finished. "O.K. Thanks, Mary."

He switched off and sat thinking. Somewhere in the bowels of the Body Administrative, he knew, notations were being made and cross-filed. The addition of Karlshaven IV to the list of planets under colonization would be made, and Holliday's asking prices for land would be posted with Emigration, together with a prospectus abstracted from the General Galactic Survey.

He switched the interphone on again.

"Uh ... Mary? Supply me with a copy of the GenSurv on the entire Karlshaven system. Tell Mr. Mead I'll expect him in my office sometime this afternoon—you schedule it—and we'll go into it further."

"Yes, Mr. Secretary. Will fifteen-fifteen be all right?"

"Fifteen-fifteen's fine, uh ... Mary," Marlowe said gently.

"Yes, sir," his secretary replied, abashed. "I keep forgetting about proper nomenclature."

"So do I, Mary, so do I," Marlowe sighed. "Anything come up that wasn't scheduled for today?"

It was a routine question, born of futile hope. There was always something to spoil the carefully planned daily schedules.

"Yes and no, sir."

Marlowe cocked an eyebrow at the interphone.

"Well, that's a slight change, anyway. What is it?"

"There's a political science observer from Dovenil—that's Moore II on our maps, sir—who's requested permission to talk to you. He's here on the usual exchange program, and he's within his privileges in asking, of course. I assume it's the ordinary thing—what's our foreign policy, how do you apply it, can you give specific instances, and the like."

Precisely, Marlowe thought. For ordinary questions there were standard answers, and Mary had been his secretary for so long that she could supply them as well as he could.

Dovenil. Moore II, eh? Obviously, there was something special about the situation, and Mary was leaving the decision to him. He scanned through his memorized star catalogues, trying to find the correlation.

"Mr. Secretary?"

Marlowe grunted. "Still here. Just thinking. Isn't Dovenil that nation we just sent Harrison to?"

"Yes, sir. On the same exchange program."

Marlowe chuckled. "Well, if we've got Harrison down there, it's only fair to let their fellow learn something in exchange, isn't it? What's his name?"

"Dalish ud Klavan, sir."

Marlowe muttered to himself: "Dalish ud Klavan, Irish, corn beef and cabbage." His mind filed it away together with a primary-color picture of Jiggs and Maggie.

"All right, Mary, I'll talk to him, if you can find room in the schedule somewhere. Tell you what—let him in at fifteen-thirty. Mead and I can furnish a working example for him. Does that check all right with your book?"

"Yes, sir. There'll be time if we carry over on the Ceroii incidents."

"Ceroii's waited six years, four months, and twenty-three days. They'll wait another day. Let's do that, then, uh ... Mary."

"Yes, sir."

Marlowe switched off and picked up a report which he began to read by the page-block system, his eyes almost unblinking between pages. "Harrison, eh?" he muttered once, stopping to look quizzically at his desktop. He chuckled.

At fifteen-fifteen, the light on his interphone blinked twice, and Marlowe hastily initialed a directive with his right hand while touching the switch with his left.

"Yes, Mary?"

"Mr. Mead, sir."

"O.K." He switched off, pushed the directive into his OUT box, and pulled the GenSurv and the folder on Martin Holliday out of the HOLD tray. "Come in, Chris," he said as Mead knocked on the door.

"How are you today, Mr. Marlowe?" Mead asked as he sat down.

"Four ounces heavier," Marlowe answered dryly. "I presume you're not. Cigarette, Chris?"

Apparently, the use of the first name finally caught Mead's notice. He looked thoughtful for a moment, then took a cigarette and lit it. "Thanks—Dave."

"Well, I'm glad that's settled," Marlowe chuckled, his eyes almost disappearing in crinkles of flesh. "How's Mary?"

Mead grinned crookedly. "Miss Folsom is in fine fettle today, thank you."

Marlowe rumbled a laugh. Mead had once made the mistake of addressing the woman as "Mary," under the natural assumption that if Marlowe could do it, everyone could.

"Mary, I fear," Marlowe observed, "lives in more stately times than these. She'll tolerate informality from me because I'm in direct authority over her, and direct authority, of course, is Law. But you, Mead, are a young whipper-snapper."

"But that's totally unrealistic!" Mead protested. "I don't respect her less by using her first name ... it's just ... just friendliness, that's all."

"Look," Marlowe said, "it makes sense, but it ain't logical—not on her terms. Mary Folsom was raised by a big, tough, tight-lipped authoritarian of a father who believed in bringing kids up by the book. By the time she got tumbled out into the world, all big men were unquestionable authority and all young men were callow whipper-snappers. Sure, she's unhappy about it, inside. But it makes her a perfect secretary, for me, and she does her job well. We play by her rules on the little things, and by the world's rules on the big ones. Kapish?"

"Sure, Dave, but—"

Marlowe picked up the folder on Holliday and gave Mead one weighty but understanding look before he opened it.

"Your trouble, Chris, is that your viewpoint is fundamentally sane," he said. "Now, about Holliday, Martin, options 062-26-8729, 063-108-1004. I didn't get time to read the GenSurv on the Karlshaven planets, so I'll ask you to brief me."

"Yes, sir."

"What's IV like?"

"Good, arable land. A little mountainous in spots, but that's good. Loaded with minerals—industrial stuff, like silver. Some tin, but not enough to depress the monetary standard. Lots of copper. Coal beds, petroleum basins, the works. Self-supporting practically from the start, a real asset to the Union in fifty-six years."

Marlowe nodded. "Good. Nice picking, Chris. Now—got a decoy?"

"Yes, sir. Karlshaven II's a False-E. I've got a dummy option on it in the works, and we'll be able to undercut Holliday's prices for his land by about twenty per cent."

"False-E, huh? How long do you figure until the colony can't stick on it any longer?"

"A fair-sized one, with lots of financial backing, might even make it permanently. But we won't be able to dig up that many loafers, and, naturally, we can't give them that big a subsidy. Eventually, we'll have to ferry them all out—in about eight years, say. But that'll give us time enough to break Holliday."

Marlowe nodded again. "Sounds good."

"Something else," Mead said. "II's mineral-poor. It's near to being solid metal. That's what makes it impossible to really live on, but I figure we can switch the mineral companies right onto it and off."

Marlowe grinned approvingly. "You been saving this one for Holliday?"

"Yes, sir," Mead said, nodding slowly. He looked hesitantly at Marlowe.

"What's up, Boy?"

"Well, sir—" Mead began, then stopped. "Nothing important, really."

Marlowe gave him a surprising look full of sadness and brooding understanding.

"You're thinking he's an old, frightened man, and why don't we leave him alone?"

"Why ... yes, sir."

"Dave."

"Yes, Dave."

"You're quite right. Why don't we?"

"We can't, sir. I know that. But it doesn't seem fair—"

"Exactly, Chris. It ain't right, but it's correct."

The light on Marlowe's interphone blinked once. Marlowe looked at it in momentary surprise. Then his features cleared, and he muttered "Cabbage." He reached out toward the switch.

"We've got a visitor, Chris. Follow my lead." He reviewed his information on Dovenilid titular systems while he touched the switch. "Ask ud Klavan to come in, uh ... Mary."

Dalish ud Klavan was almost a twin for the pictured typical Dovenilid in Marlowe's library. Since the pictures were usually idealized, it followed that Klavan was an above-average specimen of his people. He stood a full eight feet from fetters to crest, and had not yet begun to thicken his shoes in compensation for the stoop that marked advancing middle age for his race.

Marlowe, looking at him, smiled inwardly. No Dovenilid could be so obviously superior and still only a lowly student. Well, considering Harrison's qualifications, it might still not be tit for tat.

Mead began to get to his feet, and Marlowe hastily planted a foot atop his nearest shoe. The assistant winced and twitched his lips, but at least he stayed down.

"Dalish ud Klavan," the Dovenilid pronounced, in good English.

"David Marlowe, Secretary for External Affairs, Solar Union," Marlowe replied.

Ud Klavan looked expectantly at Mead.

"Christopher Mead, Assistant Undersecretary for External Affairs," the assistant said, orientating himself.

"If you would do us the honor of permitting us to stand—" Marlowe asked politely.

"On the contrary, Marlowe. If you would do me the honor of permitting me to sit, I should consider it a privilege."

"Please do so. Mr. Mead, if you would bring our visitor a chair—"

They lost themselves in formalities for a few minutes, Marlowe being urbanely correct, Mead following after as best he could through the maze of Dovenilid morés. Finally they were able to get down to the business at hand, ud Klavan sitting with considerable comfort in the carefully designed chair which could be snapped into almost any shape, Marlowe bulking behind his desk, Mead sitting somewhat nervously beside him.

"Now, as I understand it, ud Klavan," Marlowe began, "you'd like to learn something of our policies and methods."

"That is correct, Marlowe and Mead." The Dovenilid extracted a block of opaque material from the flat wallet at his side and steadied it on his knee. "I have your permission to take notes?"

"Please do. Now, as it happens, Mr. Mead and I are currently considering a case which perfectly illustrates our policies."

Ud Klavan immediately traced a series of ideographs on the note block, and Marlowe wondered if he was actually going to take their conversation down verbatim. He shrugged mentally. He'd have to ask him, at some later date, whether he'd missed anything. Undoubtedly, there'd be a spare recording of the tape he himself was making.

"To begin: As you know, our government is founded upon principles of extreme personal freedom. There are no arbitrary laws governing expression, worship, the possession of personal weapons, or the rights of personal property. The state is construed to be a mechanism of public service, operated by the Body Politic, and the actual regulation and regimentation of society is accomplished by natural socio-economic laws which, of course, are both universal and unavoidable.

"We pride ourselves on the high status of the individual in comparison to the barely-tolerable existence of the state. We do, naturally, have ordinances and injunctions governing crimes, but even these are usually superseded by civil action at the personal level."

Marlowe leaned forward a trifle. "Forgetting exact principles for a moment, ud Klavan, you realize that the actuality will sometimes stray from the ideal. Our citizens, for example, do not habitually carry weapons except under extraordinary conditions. But that is a civil taboo, rather than a fixed amendation of our constitution. I have no doubt that some future generation, morés having shifted, will, for example, revive the code duello."

Ud Klavan nodded. "Quite understood, thank you, Marlowe."

"Good. Now, to proceed:

"Under conditions such as those, the state and its agencies cannot lay down a fixed policy of any sort, and expect it to be in the least permanent. The people will not tolerate such regulation, and with each new shift in social morés—and the institution of any policy is itself sufficient to produce such a shift within a short time—successive policies are repudiated by the Body Politic, and new ones must be instituted."

Marlowe leaned back and spread his hands. "Therefore," he said with a rueful smile, "it can fairly be said that we have no foreign policy, effectively speaking. We pursue the expedient, ud Klavan, and hope for the best. The case which Mr. Mead and I are currently considering is typical.

"The Union, as you know, maintains a General Survey Corps whose task it is to map the galaxy, surveying such planets as harbor alien races or seem suitable for human colonization. Such a survey team, for example, first established contact between your people and ours. Exchange observation rights are worked out, and representatives of both races are given the opportunity to acquaint themselves with the society of the other.

"In the case of unoccupied, habitable planets, however, the state's function ceases with the filing of a complete and definitive survey at the

Under-Ministry for Emigration. The state, as a state, sponsors no colonies and makes no establishments except for the few staging bases which are maintained for the use of the Survey Corps. We have not yet found any need for the institution of an offensive service analogous to a planetary army, nor do we expect to. War in space is possible only under extraordinary conditions, and we foresee no such contingency.

"All our colonization is carried out by private citizens who apply to Mr. Mead, here, for options on suitable unoccupied planets. Mr. Mead's function is to act as a consultant in these cases. He maintains a roster of surveyed human-habitable planets, and either simply assigns the requested planet or recommends one to fit specified conditions. The cost of the option is sufficient to cover the administrative effort involved, together with sufficient profit to the government to finance further surveys.

"The individual holding the option is then referred to Emigration, which provides copies of a prospectus taken from the General Survey report, and advertises the option holder's asking prices on subdivisions. Again, there is a reasonable fee of a nature similar to ours, devoted to the same purposes.

"The state then ceases to have any voice in the projected colonization whatsoever. It is a totally private enterprise—a simple real estate operation, if you will, with the state acting only as an advertising agency, and, occasionally, as the lessor of suitable transportation from Earth to the new planet. The colonists, of course, are under our protection, maintaining full citizenship unless they request independence, which is freely granted.

"If you would like to see it for purposes of clarification, you're welcome to examine our file on Martin Holliday, a citizen who is fairly typical of these real estate operators, and who has just filed an option on his second planet." Smiling, Marlowe extended the folder.

"Thank you, I should like to," ud Klavan said, and took the file from Marlowe. He leafed through it rapidly, pausing, after asking Marlowe's leave, to make notes on some of the information, and then handed it back.

"Most interesting," ud Klavan observed. "However, if you'll enlighten me—This man, Martin Holliday; wouldn't there seem to be very little incentive for him, considering his age, even if there is the expectation of a high monetary return? Particularly since his first attempt, while not a failure, was not an outstanding financial success?"

Marlowe shrugged helplessly. "I tend to agree with you thoroughly, ud Klavan, but—" he smiled, "you'll agree, I'm sure, that one Earthman's boredom is another's incentive? We are not a rigorously logical race, ud Klavan."

"Quite," the Dovenilid replied.

Marlowe stared at his irrevocable clock. His interphone light flickered, and he touched the switch absently.

"Yes, Mary?"

"Will there be anything else, Mr. Secretary?"

"No, thank you, Mary. Good night."

"Good night, sir."

There was no appeal. The day was over, and he had to go home.

He stared helplessly at his empty office, his mind automatically counting the pairs of departing footsteps that sounded momentarily as clerks and stenographers crossed the walk below his partly-open window. Finally he rolled his chair back and pushed himself to his feet. Disconsolate, he moved irresolutely to the window and watched the people leave.

Washington—aging, crowded Washington, mazed by narrow streets, carrying the burden of the severe, unimaginative past on its grimy architecture—respired heavily under the sinking sun.

The capital ought to be moved, he thought as he'd thought every night at this time. Nearer the heart of the empire. Out of this steamy bog. Out of this warren.

His heavy lips moved into an ironical comment on his own thoughts. No one was ever going to move the empire's traditional seat. There was too much nostalgia concentrated here, along with the humidity. Some day, when the Union was contiguous with the entire galaxy, men would still call Washington, on old, out-of-the-way Earth, their capital. Man was not a rigorously logical race, as a race.

The thought of going home broke out afresh, insidiously avoiding the barriers of bemusement which he had tried to erect, and he turned abruptly away from the window, moving decisively so as to be able to move at all. He yanked open a desk drawer and stuffed his jacket pockets with candy bars, ripping the film from one and chewing on its end while he put papers in his brief case.

Finally, he could not delay any longer. Everyone else was out of the building, and the robots were taking over. Metal treads spun along the corridors, bearing brooms, and the robot switchboards guarded the communications of the Ministry. Soon the char-robots would be bustling into this very office. He sighed and walked slowly out, down the empty halls where no human eye could see him waddling.

He stepped into his car, and as he opened the door the automatic recording said "Home, please," in his own voice. The car waited until he was settled and then accelerated gently, pointing for his apartment.

The recording had been an unavoidable but vicious measure of his own. He'd had to resort to it, for the temptation to drive to a terminal, to an airport, or rocket field, or railroad station—anywhere—had become excruciating.

The car stopped for a pedestrian light, and a sports model bounced jauntily to a stop beside it. The driver cocked an eyebrow at Marlowe and chuckled. "Say, Fatso, which one of you's the Buick?" Then the light changed, the car spurted away, and left Marlowe cringing.

He would not get an official car and protect himself with its license number. He would not be a coward. He would not!

His fingers shaking, he tore the film from another candy bar.

Marlowe huddled in his chair, the notebook clamped on one broad thigh by his heavy hand, his lips mumbling nervously while his pencil-point checked off meter.

"Dwell in aching discontent," he muttered. "No. Not that." He stared down at the floor, his eyes distant.

"Bitter discontent," he whispered. He grunted softly with breath that had to force its way past the constricting weight of his hunched chest. "Bitter dwell." He crossed out the third line, substituted the new one, and began to read the first two verses to himself.

"We are born of Humankind—
This our destiny:
To bitter dwell in discontent
Wherever we may be.

"To strangle with the burden
Of that which heels us on.
To stake our fresh beginnings
When frailer breeds have done."

He smiled briefly, content. It still wasn't perfect, but it was getting closer. He continued:

"To pile upon the ashes
Of races in decease
Such citadels of our kind's own
As fortify no—"

"What are you doing, David?" his wife asked over his shoulder.

Flinching, he pulled the notebook closer into his lap, bending forward in an instinctive effort to protect it.

The warm, loving, sawing voice went on. "Are you writing another poem, David? Why, I thought you'd given that up!"

"It's ... it's nothing, really, uh ... Leonora. Nothing much. Just a ... a thing I've had running around my head. Wanted to get rid of it."

His wife leaned over and kissed his cheek clumsily. "Why, you old big dear! I'll bet it's for me. Isn't it, David? Isn't it for me?"

He shook his head in almost desperate regret. "I'm ... I'm afraid not, uh—" Snorer. "It's about something else, Leonora."

"Oh." She came around the chair, and he furtively wiped his cheek with a hasty hand. She sat down facing him, smiling with entreaty. "Would you read it to me anyway, David? Please, dear?"

"Well, it's not ... not finished yet—not right."

"You don't have to, David. It's not important. Not really." She sighed deeply.

He picked up the notebook, his breath cold in his constricted throat. "All right," he said, the words coming out huskily, "I'll read it. But it's not finished yet."

"If you don't want to—"

He began to read hurriedly, his eyes locked on the notebook, his voice a suppressed hoarse, spasmodic whisper.

"Such citadels of our kind's own
As fortify no peace.
"No wall can offer shelter,
No roof can shield from pain.
We cannot rest; we are the damned;
We must go forth again.
"Unnumbered we must—"

"David, are you sure about those last lines?" She smiled apologetically. "I know I'm old-fashioned, but couldn't you change that? It seems so ... so harsh. And I think you may have unconsciously borrowed it from someone else. I can't help thinking I've heard it before, somewhere? Don't you think so?"

"I don't know, dear. You may be right about that word, but it doesn't really matter, does it? I mean,

I'm not going to try to get it published, or anything."

"I know, dear, but still—"

He was looking at her desperately.

"I'm sorry, dear!" she said contritely. "Please go on. Don't pay any attention to my stupid comments."

"They're not stupid—"

"Please, dear. Go on."

His fingers clamped on the edge of the notebook.

"Unnumbered we must wander,
Break, and bleed, and die.
Implacable as ocean,
Our tide must drown the sky.

"What is our expiation,
For what primeval crime,
That we must go on marching
Until the crash of time?

"What hand has shaped so cruelly?
What whim has cast such fate?
Where is, in our creation,
The botch that makes us great?"

"Oh, that's good, darling! That's very good. I'm proud of you, David."

"I think it stinks," he said evenly, "but, anyway, there are two more verses."

"David!"

Grimly, he spat out the last eight lines.

"Why are we ever gimleted
By empire's irony?
Is discontent the cancered price

Of Earthman's galaxy?"

Leonora, recoiling from his cold fury, was a shaking pair of shoulders and a mass of lank hair supported by her hands on her face while she sobbed.

"Are our souls so much perverted?
Can we not relent?
Or are the stars the madman's cost
For his inborn discontent?
"Good night, Leonora."

The light flickered on Marlowe's interphone.

"Good morning, Mr. Secretary."

"Good morning, Mary. What's up?"

"Harrison's being deported from Dovenil, sir. There's a civil crime charged against him. Quite a serious one."

Marlowe's eyebrows went up. "How much have we got on it?"

"Not too much, sir. Harrison's report hasn't come in yet. But the story's on the news broadcasts now, sir. We haven't been asked to comment yet, but Emigration has been called by several news outlets, and the Ministry for Education just called here and inquired whether it would be all right to publish a general statement of their exchange students' careful instructions against violating local customs."

Marlowe's glance brooded down on the mass of papers piled in the tray of his IN box. "Give me a tape of a typical broadcast," he said at last. "Hold everything else. Present explanation to all news outlets: None now, statement forthcoming after preliminary investigation later in the day. The Ministry regrets this incident deeply, and will try to settle matters as soon and as amicably as possible, et cetera, et cetera. O.K.?"

"Yes, sir."

He swung his chair around to face the screen let into a side wall, and colors began to flicker and run in the field almost immediately. They steadied and sharpened, and the broadcast tape began to roll.

Dateline: Dovenil, Sector Three, Day 183, 2417 GST. Your Topical News reporter on this small planet at the Union's rim was unable today to locate for comment any of the high officials of this alien civilization directly concerned with the order for the deportation of exchange student-observer Hubert Harrison, charged with theft and violent assault on the person of a Dovenilid citizen. Union citizen Harrison was unavailable for comment at this time, but Topical News will present his views and such other clues when more ensues.

Marlowe grunted. Journalese was getting out of hand again. That last rhyming sentence was sure to stick in the audience's brains. It might be only another advertising gimmick, but if they started doing it with the body of the news itself, it might be well to feed Topical enough false leads to destroy what little reputation for comprehensibility they had left.

He touched his interphone switch.

"Uh ... Mary, what was the hooper on that broadcast?"

"Under one per cent, sir."

Which meant that, so far, the Body Politic hadn't reacted.

"Thank you. Is there anything else coming in?"

"Not at the moment, sir."

"What's—" Cabbage. "What's Dalish ud Klavan doing?"

"His residence is the Solar Hostel, sir. The management reports that he is still in his room, and has not reserved space on any form of long-distance transportation. He has not contacted us, either, and there is a strong probability that he may still be unaware of what's happened."

"How many calls did he make yesterday, either before or after he was here, and to whom?"

"I can get you a list in ten minutes, sir."

"Do that, Mary."

He switched off, sat slapping the edge of his desk with his hand, and switched on again.

"Mary, I want the GenSurvs on the Dovenil area to a depth of ten cubic lights."

"Yes, sir."

"And get me Mr. Mead on the phone, please."

"Yes, sir."

Marlowe's lips pulled back from his teeth as he switched off. He snatched a candy bar out of his drawer, tore the film part way off, then threw it back in the drawer as his desk phone chimed.

"Here, Chris."

"Here, Mr. Marlowe."

"Look, Chris—has Holliday left Earth yet?"

"Yes, sir. Yes, Dave."

"Where is he?"

"Luna, en route to Karlshaven. He was lucky enough to have me arrange for his accidentally getting a ride on a GenSurv ship that happened to be going out that way, if you follow me." Mead grinned.

"Get him back."

The smile blanked out. "I can't do that, Mr. Marlowe! He'd never be able to take it. You should have seen him when I put him on the shuttle. We doped him up with EasyRest, and even then his subconscious could feel the bulkheads around him, even in his sleep. Those shuttles are small, and they don't have ports."

"We can't help that. We need him, and I've got to talk to him first. Personally."

Mead bit his lip. "Yes, sir."

"Dave."

"Yes ... Dave."

Dalish ud Klavan sat easily in his chair opposite Marlowe. He rested one digit on his notebook and waited.

"Ud Klavan," Marlowe said amiably, "you're undoubtedly aware by now that your opposite number on Dovenil has been charged with a civil crime and deported."

The Dovenilid nodded. "An unfortunate incident. One that I regret personally, and which I am sure my own people would much rather not have had happen."

"Naturally." Marlowe smiled. "I simply wanted to reassure you that this incident does not reflect on your own status in any way. We are investigating our representative, and will take appropriate action, but it seems quite clear that the fault is not with your people. We have already forwarded reparations and a note of apology to your government. As further reparation, I wish to assure you personally that we will coöperate with your personal observations in every possible way. If there is anything at all you wish to know—even what might, under ordinary conditions, be considered restricted information—just call on us."

Ud Klavan's crest stirred a fraction of an inch, and Marlowe chuckled inwardly. Well, even a brilliant spy might be forgiven an outward display of surprise under these circumstances.

The Dovenilid gave him a piercing look, but Marlowe presented a featureless facade of bulk.

The secretary chuckled in his mind once more. He doubted if ud Klavan could accept the hypothesis that Marlowe did not know he was a spy. But the Dovenilid must be a sorely confused being at this point.

"Thank you, Marlowe," he said finally. "I am most grateful, and I am sure my people will construe it as yet another sign of the Union's friendship."

"I hope so, ud Klavan," Marlowe replied. Having exchanged this last friendly lie, they went through the customary Dovenilid formula of leave-taking.

Marlowe slapped his interphone switch as soon as the alien was gone. "Uh ... Mary, what's the latest on Holliday?"

"His shuttle lands at Idlewild in half an hour, sir."

"All right, get Mr. Mead. Have him meet me out front, and get an official car to take us to the field. I'll want somebody from Emigration to go with us. Call Idlewild and have them set up a desk and chairs for four out in the middle of the field. Call the Ministry for Traffic and make sure that field stays clear until we're through with it. My Ministerial prerogative, and no back-talk. I want that car in ten minutes."

"Yes, sir."

Mary's voice was perfectly even, without the slightest hint that there was anything unusual happening. Marlowe switched off and twisted his mouth.

He picked up the GenSurv on the Dovenil area and began skimming it rapidly.

He kept his eyes carefully front as he walked out of his office, past the battery of clerks in the outer office, and down the hall. He kept them rigidly fixed on the door of his personal elevator which, during the day, was human-operated under the provisions of the Human Employment Act of 2302. He met Mead in front of the building and did not look into the eyes of Bussard, the man from Emigration, as they shook hands. He followed them down the walk in a sweating agony of obliviousness, and climbed into the car with carefully normal lack of haste.

He sat sweating, chewing a candy bar, for several minutes before he spoke. Then, slowly, he felt his battered defenses reassert themselves, and he could actually look at Bussard, before he turned to Mead.

"Now, then," he rapped out a shade too abruptly before he caught himself. "Here's the GenSurv on the Dovenil area, Chris. Anything in it you don't know already?"

"I don't think so, sir."

"O.K., dig me up a habitable planet—even a long-term False-E will do—close to Dovenil, but not actually in their system. If it's at all possible, I want that world in a system without any rich planets. And I don't want any rich systems anywhere near it. If you can't do that, arrange for the outright sale of all mineral and other resource rights to suitable companies. I want that planet to be habitable, but I want it to be impossible for any people on it to get at enough resources to achieve a technological culture. Can do?"

Mead shook his head. "I don't know."

"You've got about fifteen minutes to find out. I'm going to start talking to Holliday, and when I tell him I've got another planet for him, I'll be depending on you to furnish one. Sorry to pile it on like this, but must be."

Mead nodded. "Right, Mr. Marlowe. That's why I draw pay."

"Good boy. Now, uh—" Rabbit. "Bussard. I want you to be ready to lay out a complete advertising and prospectus program. Straight routine work, but about four times normal speed. The toughest part of it will be following the lead that Chris and I set. Don't be surprised at anything, and act like it happens every day."

"Yes, Mr. Marlowe."

"Right."

Bussard looked uncomfortable. "Ah ... Mr. Marlowe?"

"Yes?"

"About this man, Harrison. I presume all this is the result of what happened to him on Dovenil. Do you think there's any foundation in truth for what they say he did? Or do you think it's just an excuse to get him off their world?"

Marlowe looked at him coldly. "Don't be an ass," he snorted.

Martin Holliday climbed slowly out of the shuttle's lock and moved fumblingly down the stairs, leaning on the attendant's arm. His face was a mottled gray, and his hands shook uncontrollably. He stepped down to the tarmac and his head turned from side to side as his eyes gulped the field's distances.

Marlowe sat behind the desk that had been put down in the middle of this emptiness, his eyes brooding as he looked at Holliday. Bussard stood beside him, trying nervously to appear noncommittal, while Mead went up to the shaking old man, grasped his hand, and brought him over to the desk.

Marlowe shifted uncomfortably. The desk was standard size, and he had to sit far away from it. He could not feel at ease in such a position.

His thick fingers went into the side pocket of his jacket and peeled the film off a candy bar, and he began to eat it, holding it in his left hand, as Mead introduced Holliday.

"How do you do, Mr. Holliday?" Marlowe said, his voice higher than he would have liked it, while he shook the man's hand.

"I'm ... I'm pleased to meet you, Mr. Secretary," Holliday replied. His eyes were darting past Marlowe's head.

"This is Mr. Bussard, of Emigration, and you know Mr. Mead, of course. Now, I think we can all sit down."

Mead's chair was next to Holliday's, and Bussard's was to one side of the desk, so that only Marlowe, unavoidably, blocked his complete view of the stretching tarmac.

"First of all, Mr. Holliday, I'd like to thank you for coming back. Please believe me when I say we would not have made such a request if it were not urgently necessary."

"It's all right," Holliday said in a low, apologetic voice. "I don't mind."

Marlowe winced, but he had to go on.

"Have you seen a news broadcast recently, Mr. Holliday?"

The man shook his head in embarrassment. "No, sir. I've been ... asleep most of the time."

"I understand, Mr. Holliday. I didn't really expect you had under the circumstances. The situation is this:

"Some time ago, our survey ships, working out in their usual expanding pattern, encountered an alien civilization on a world designated Moore II on our maps, and which the natives call Dovenil. It was largely a routine matter, no different from any other alien contact which we've had. They had a relatively high technology, embracing the beginnings of interplanetary flight, and our contact teams were soon able to work out a diplomatic status mutually satisfactory to both.

"Social observers were exchanged, in accordance with the usual practice, and everything seemed to be going well."

Holliday nodded out of painful politeness, not seeing the connection with himself. Some of his nervousness was beginning to fade, but it was impossible for him to be really at ease with so many people near him, with all of Earth's billions lurking at the edge of the tarmac.

"However," Marlowe went on as quickly as he could, "today, our representative was deported on a trumped-up charge. Undoubtedly, this is only the first move in some complicated scheme directed against the Union. What it is, we do not yet know, but further observation of the actions of their own representative on this planet has convinced us that they are a clever, ruthless people, living in a society which would have put Machiavelli to shame. They are single-minded of purpose, and welded into a tight group whose major purpose in life is the service of the state in its major purpose, which, by all indications, is that of eventually dominating the universe.

"You know our libertarian society. You know that the Union government is almost powerless, and that the Union itself is nothing but a loose federation composed of a large number of independent nations tied together by very little more than the fact that we are all Earthmen.

"We are almost helpless in the face of such a nation as the Dovenilids. They have already outmaneuvered us once, despite our best efforts. There is no sign that they will not be able to do so again, at will.

"We must, somehow, discover what the Dovenilids intend to do next. For this reason, I earnestly request that you accept our offer of another planet than the one you have optioned, closer to the Dovenilid system. We are willing, under these extraordinary circumstances, to consider your credit sufficient for the outright purchase of half the planet, and Mr. Bussard, here, will do his utmost to get you suitable colonists for the other half as rapidly as it can be done. Will you help us, Mr. Holliday?"

Marlowe sank back in his chair. He became conscious of a messy feeling in his left hand, and looked down to discover the half-eaten candy bar had melted. He tried furtively to wipe his hand clean on the underside of the desk, but he knew Bussard had noticed, and he cringed and cursed himself.

Holliday's face twisted nervously.

"I ... I don't know—"

"Please don't misunderstand us, Mr. Holliday," Marlowe said. "We do not intend to ask you to spy for us, nor are we acting with the intention of now establishing a base of any sort on the planet. We simply would like to have a Union world near the

Dovenilid system. Whatever Dovenil does will not have gathered significant momentum by the end of your life. You will be free to end your days exactly as you have always wished, and the precautions we have outlined will ensure that there will be no encroachments on your personal property during that time. We are planning for the next generation, when Dovenil will be initiating its program of expansion. It is then that we will need an established outpost near their borders."

"Yes," Holliday said hesitantly, "I can understand that. I ... I don't know," he repeated. "It seems all right. And, as you say, it won't matter, during my lifetime, and it's more than I had really hoped for." He looked nervously at Mead. "What do you think, Mr. Mead? You've always done your best for me."

Mead shot one quick glance at Marlowe. "I think Mr. Marlowe's doing his best for the Union," he said finally, "and I know he is fully aware of your personal interests. I think what he's doing is reasonable under the circumstances, and I think his proposition to you, as he's outlined it, is something which you cannot afford to not consider. The final decision is up to you, of course."

Holliday nodded slowly, staring down at his hands. "Yes, yes, I think you're right, Mr. Mead." He looked up at Marlowe. "I'll be glad to help. And I'm grateful for the consideration you've shown me."

"Not at all, Mr. Holliday. The Union is in your debt."

Marlowe wiped his hand on the underside of the desk again, but he only made matters worse, for his fingers picked up some of the chocolate he had removed before.

"Mr. Mead, will you give Mr. Holliday the details on the new planet?" he said, trying to get his handkerchief out without smearing his suit. He could almost hear Bussard snickering.

Holliday signed the new option contract and shook Marlowe's hand. "I'd like to thank you again, sir. Looking at it from my point of view, it's something for nothing—at least, while I'm alive. And it's a very nice planet, too, from the way Mr. Mead described it. Even better than Karlshaven."

"Nevertheless, Mr. Holliday," Marlowe said, "you have done the Union a great service. We would consider it an honor if you allowed us to enter your planet in our records under the name of Holliday."

He kept his eyes away from Mead.

Martin Holliday's eyes were shining. "Thank you, Mr. Marlowe," he said huskily.

Marlowe could think of no reply. Finally, he simply nodded. "It's been a pleasure meeting you, Mr. Holliday. We've arranged transportation, and your shuttle will be taking off very shortly."

Holliday's face began to bead with fresh perspiration at the thought of bulkheads enclosing him once more, but he managed to smile, and then ask, hesitantly: "May I ... may I wait for the shuttle out here, sir?"

"Certainly. We'll arrange for that. Well, good-by, Mr. Holliday."

"Good-by, Mr. Marlowe. Good-by, Mr. Bussard. And good-by, Mr. Mead. I don't suppose you'll be seeing me again."

"Good luck, Mr. Holliday," Mead said.

Marlowe twisted awkwardly on the car's back seat, wiping futilely at the long smear of chocolate on his trouser pocket.

Well, he thought, at least he'd given the old man his name on the star maps until Earthmen stopped roving.

At least he'd given him that.

Mead was looking at him. "I don't suppose we've got time to let him die in peace, have we?" he asked.

Marlowe shook his head.

"I suppose we'll have to start breaking him immediately, won't we?"

Marlowe nodded.

"I'll get at it right away, sir."

Dave! Does everyone have to hate me? Can't anyone understand? Even you, uh—Creed. Even you, Mead?

Dalish ud Klavan, stooped and withered, sat hopelessly, opposite Marlowe, who sat behind his desk like a grizzled polar bear, his thinning mane of white hair unkempt and straggling.

"Marlowe, my people are strangling," the old Dovenilid said.

Marlowe looked at him silently.

"The Holliday Republic has signed treaty after treaty with us, and still their citizens raid our mining planets, driving away our own people, stealing the resources we must have if we are to live."

Marlowe sighed. "There's nothing I can do."

"We have gone to the Holliday government repeatedly," ud Klavan pleaded. "They tell us the raiders are criminals, that they are doing their best to stop them. But they still buy the metal the raiders bring them."

"They have to," Marlowe said. "There are no available resources anywhere within practicable distances. If they're to have any civilization at all, they've got to buy from the outlaws."

"But they are members of the Union!" ud Klavan protested. "Why won't you do anything to stop them?"

"We can't," Marlowe said again. "They're members of the Union, yes, but they're also a free republic. We have no administrative jurisdiction over them, and if we attempted to establish one our citizens would rise in protest all over our territory."

"Then we're finished. Dovenil is a dead world."

Marlowe nodded slowly. "I am very sorry. If there is anything I can do, or that the Ministry can do, we will do it. But we cannot save the Dovenilid state."

Ud Klavan looked at him bitterly. "Thank you," he said. "Thank you for your generous offer of a gracious funeral.

"I don't understand you!" he burst out suddenly. "I don't understand you people! Diplomatic lies, yes. Expediency, yes! But this ... this madness, this fanatical, illogical devotion of the state in the cause of a people who will tolerate no state! This ... no, this I cannot understand."

Marlowe looked at him, his eyes full of years.

"Ud Klavan," he said, "you are quite right. We are a race of maniacs. And that is why Earthmen rule the galaxy. For our treaties are not binding, and our promises are worthless. Our government does not represent our people. It represents our people as they once were. The delay in the democratic process is such that the treaty signed today fulfills the promise of yesterday—but today the Body Politic has formed a new opinion, is following a new logic which is completely at variance with that of yesterday. An Earthman's promise—expressed in words or deeds—is good only at the instant he makes it. A second later, new factors have entered into the total circumstances, and a new chain of logic has formed in his head—to be altered again, a few seconds later."

He thought, suddenly, of that poor claustrophobic devil, Holliday, harried from planet to planet, never given a moment's rest—and civilizing, civilizing, spreading the race of humankind wherever he was driven. Civilizing with a fervor no hired dummy could have accomplished, driven by his fear to sell with all the real estate agent's talent that had been born in him, selling for the sake of money with which to buy that land he needed for his peace—and always being forced to sell a little too much.

Ud Klavan rose from his chair. "You are also right, Marlowe. You are a race of maniacs, gibbering across the stars. And know, Marlowe, that the other races of the universe hate you."

Marlowe with a tremendous effort heaved himself out of his chair.

"Hate us?" He lumbered around the desk and advanced on the frightened Dovenilid, who was retreating backwards before his path.

"Can't you see it? Don't you understand that, if we are to pursue any course of action over a long time—if we are ever going to achieve a galaxy in which an Earthman can some day live at peace with himself—we must each day violate all the moral codes and creeds which we held inviolate the day before? That we must fight against every ideal, every principle which our fathers taught us, because they no longer apply to our new logic?

"You hate us!" He thrust his fat hand, its nails bitten down to the quick and beyond, in front of the cringing alien's eyes.

"You poor, weak, single-minded, ineffectual thing! We hate ourselves!"